About the Book

Almost since Joe could remember, the Coaltown mines had been closed. The men who had not moved their families to the city stuck it out hoping for a miracle that would reopen them. And Joe Novak's Dad was one of them.

Christmas was the hardest time of year, but at least this year, the Novaks had the tallest tree in town and Joe could take it to the tree-burning festival at the end of Christmas. But this was no ordinary tree—at least that's what Grandma said—and she proved she was right.

Dale Fife has created a warm and unusual story about family life and loyalties, and Margot Tomes captures the mood in her distinctive illustrations.

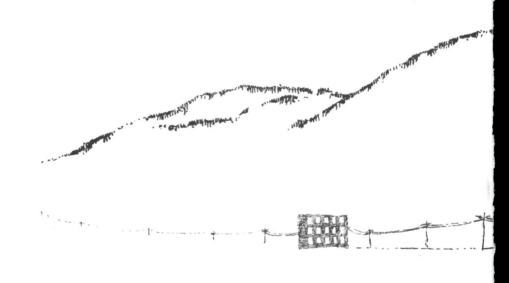

Coward-McCann, Inc.   New York

JOE *and the* TALKING CHRISTMAS TREE

BY DALE FIFE
Illustrated by Margot Tomes

To Gertrude Farrell
of
Old Mauch Chunk

Joe Novak ran and slid by turns down the icy sidewalk of his hilly street, noticing, but not stopping this night, to look at the lighted trees in the windows of the miners' cottages. Almost everyone in Lower Coaltown was poor again this Christmas because the mines were still closed. Yet most had managed to buy some kind of tree.

The Novak cottage was the last one before the thick woods. Its front window was dark. But it wouldn't be for long. Not if Pop had money. To-

night was Christmas Eve when the leftover trees sold cheaply. Joe had gone Overtown, which was what the people called Upper Coaltown, hoping to get a job shoveling snow in front of one of the stores. The merchants weren't hiring this year. Business was too bad. Joe wanted a big tree, and he had hoped to help out. This year he wanted one at least as tall as his Cousin Karl would have, to take to the New Year's Eve fire. At the thought of his braggart Cousin Karl, Joe's chin went out.

The Novaks always used the back door, and now Joe scooted around the side path to the storm porch, where he shook the snow from his jacket and stamped it from his rubbers before bursting into the kitchen.

Grandma was standing at the square kitchen-dining table, ladling soup into bowls from a tureen. "Well, and who is this late one?" she asked. "He must not wish to go Overtown to pick out a tree."

A feeling of warm well-being washed over Joe. Grandma was telling him there was no question about the tree. Grandma was saucy and quick, even though she was so old that her face was a crisscross of wrinkles and she was almost toothless. Her hair, which she braided and wound in two big circles over her ears, was not gray. She reminded Joe of a busy little sparrow.

9

Mom was just spooning the last of the baby's cereal into his mouth. "Wash up, Joe," she said, her eyes resting gently on him.

Six-year-old Anna was already at the table, her cheeks red with excitement, her dark beribboned braids bouncing on her shoulders. Grandma gave her a little shove. "Your papa is not sitting yet. Go call him."

"Hurry, hurry, hurry," Anna shouted, running into the living room, "or all the trees will be gone."

Joe washed his hands, and then he came over to the baby and leaned across his high chair. "Wait until you see the tree lights," he said. "You won't chew on this old spoon."

The baby grabbed a fistful of Joe's hair.

"Ouch," Joe cried and made such an exaggerated face that the baby laughed gleefully.

"I want a tree as high as the ceiling," Anna shouted, running back to her place at the table. "Joe, will there be any big ones left?"

"Maybe," Joe said cautiously. Just this once he wished they would not have to settle for a runt of a tree. He'd like to take a really big tree to the New Year's Eve fire.

Pop came into the kitchen and took his place at the head of the table. "Tree, tree, that's all I

10

hear," he said. "Maybe we stay home. Maybe we don't go Overtown tonight."

"Pop," Anna screeched.

"Pop," Joe groaned.

But they knew he was teasing.

Pop was tall and strong, with thick black hair, like Joe's, and wide shoulders. He was a coal miner. But with the mines closed, he had to find whatever jobs he could. Last week he worked a day and a half repairing machinery in the silk mill Overtown. Joe linked good times with Pop coming home from the colliery, his blue eyes, red lips, and white teeth flashing in coal-blackened face. Joe knew it was hard these days for Mom to make the money stretch from one week to another.

Grandma's place at the table was between the baby's high chair and Joe. She pinched Joe's arm as she passed him. The pinch meant "You're my boy." Joe loved her. She talked a great deal about the Old Country, and tonight was no different. "In the Old Country we went with our father into the forest to pick tree," she said. "Papa, he chop it down himself. Then we hurry with tree to our home, so none of its good luck run out and be lost."

"Well, we can't do that here," Pop said. "The Old Man owns the woods."

11

"He'd chop our heads off," Anna said, shivering.

The Old Man was Feodor Petrof, who also owned the mines. He had not been in Coaltown for a long while now. He spent most of the time in some warm place where there were palm trees. Joe had never seen him, but he had grown up knowing that they were poor because the Old Man had shut down the mines.

Pop sighed. "Our Cousin Alex will be home for Christmas. I will speak to him then about my chances of getting work in the city."

Mom's hand went to her throat. Joe suddenly felt all hollow inside.

Cousin Alex was Pop's second cousin. He had gone to work in the city almost a year ago. "Until the mines open up again," he had said. Once a month he came home to see his family. Now Karl, his son, had spending money, but he ran around the streets of Coaltown and acted like a tough.

If Pop went to work in the city, he would come home just once in a while, or maybe they all would move there. Joe liked Coaltown. Here he had cousins and uncles and aunts. He loved them all, except maybe Cousin Karl, who was really only a third cousin. He was Joe's age, eight going on nine. Joe wondered if he'd change as Karl had if Pop went away. Would he sass his mother, skip school, and pick fights?

12

Now Joe no longer felt hungry. He saw Grandma glaring from one to another, her gaze finally resting on him. "It seems there are those at this table who do not taste how thick and golden with onions the soup is, how warm is the house. They do not seem to know that it is the night before Christmas, and soon there will be a tree. They do not even know that a green tree in the house brings luck."

Everyone sat up straighter.

"Merry Christmas," Anna cried.

"Don't be in such a hurry," Joe said.

They began to laugh and to eat.

Joe wanted to hug Grandma.

Soon they were ready to go Overtown, bundled into heavy coats and boots, Mom with a scarf covering her golden hair.

"I stay behind and watch the baby," Grandma said, hurrying them on their way. "Remember to shake the tree before you buy. A lucky one holds onto its needles."

"Now, Ma, let's not have any of those superstitions," Pop said, but tonight he was smiling.

Grandma had brought her superstitions with her from the Old Country. It was the one thing that Pop and Grandma argued about.

Coaltown was cupped in a heavily wooded valley. Scrub oak, maple, and pine trees spilled down

the hills to the very edge of town. The river sliced the town into Lowertown, where the miners lived, and Overtown, where the shops and some of the bigger houses were. The bridge laced the two parts together again.

"Look, look, look," Anna cried as soon as they were over the bridge and could see the courthouse tree lit up.

Next, she ran ahead to see the Nativity scene in front of the church, and Joe ran behind her. Real people played the parts of the shepherds and the wise men. Joe recognized the shoe merchant and Gus, the baker, behind their long beards. But he didn't tell Anna. Three sheep and a cow from one of the nearby farms stood in the stable alongside the crib. But to Anna, whose eyes were round with excitement, it was all straight from Bethlehem.

The church bells began to ring the Angelus. Six o'clock. Now they must hurry.

The Christmas trees were always sold on the wide cobblestoned square in front of the railroad depot. Joe saw immediately that the leftover trees were a scraggly lot.

"I didn't buy expensive ones this year," Hans Shumaker, the treeman said, pulling at his mustache with mittened fingers. "I was afraid maybe I get stuck with them."

Pop nodded. "Looks like it was just another rumor that the Old Man might reopen the mines."

"Yah! I think maybe they be closed for good. The Old Man, he like life where it is easy, nice, and warm, no snow," Hans said, stamping his feet against the cold.

Joe didn't remember, clearly, when the mines had been open full time, but he knew that whatever the Novaks, or their relations and neighbors, could not afford was due to the mines being closed.

16

When Pop's cap with the lantern and his lunch bucket with the lid that held coffee stayed on the pantry shelf, there was no use looking into store windows even at Christmastime.

Listening to the discouraging talk of the men gave Joe the hollow, scared feeling again. "Let's find us a tree," he said to Anna, and the two of them raced around from one end of the lot to the other. All the trees were rejects. Last year, for fifty cents, Pop had bought a misshapen tree, thick in spots, bare in others. He had bored holes into its trunk and fitted the bare spots with branches from the thick side. The tree looked fine when it was finished. But these trees were hopeless.

They had reached the end of the lot and were ready to turn back when Joe spotted a tall tree standing alone in the shadows against the board fence. He went closer. It was a blue hemlock with branches that tapered evenly from tip to bushy base. "Pop. Mom," he called.

Pop let out a whistle when he saw it.

Mom bent to inhale its fragrance.

Joe shook it. The needles held.

"It's three times as tall as I am," Anna said. "It will reach the ceiling."

"How much?" Pop asked, hesitatingly.

"One dollar," Hans said promptly.

17

Only one dollar. Joe couldn't believe it. Even on Christmas Eve a tree like this was expensive.

Pop's hand went quickly to his pocket. Just as quickly he withdrew it. The smile left his face. "Why just one dollar? Because I am your old friend and you know I have had little work?"

Joe held his breath. Maybe they wouldn't get the tree after all.

"You are a proud man," Hans said. "But now I will show you why the tree is one dollar and why the woman who put deposit on it refused to take it today." He carried the tree away from the fence and turned it around to face the streetlight. From the top to the bottom, across the back branches, there was a streak of yellow paint.

"How did that happen?" Mom asked.

"I have heard it is a sign in the forest. I do not know what it mean," Hans said.

Mom circled the tree. "We have enough tinsel to cover the paint. We can stand the yellow side next to the wall."

Pop put his hand in his pocket once more, and now the tree was theirs to carry home. Pop and Mom took hold of it at the middle because their arms were longest. Anna held the tip and Joe the base. It wasn't that heavy, but it was so beautiful they didn't want to risk any of its branches dragging and maybe breaking. Snowflakes drifted down. Mom started singing a carol. She had a sweet voice that sounded like bells ringing in the cold air. They all joined in, and they sang and laughed their way up and down the slippery hills to home.

Grandma had the dishes washed, the baby in bed, and the Christmas decorations out of the boxes when they marched triumphantly into the house with the magnificent tree.

"The king of the forest," Grandma said, beaming. But when she saw the painted branches, her hands flew to her cheeks, and she rolled her eyes. "It is omen."

"It's got to be a good omen with such a good tree," Joe said.

"Now, Ma, this isn't the Old Country," Pop said. "We don't believe in stuff like omens."

"I get to put the bell on," Anna said. "Where's the tinkling bell?"

And so they started, and when the tree was trimmed with ornaments saved through the years and it was garlanded with popcorn and cranberry strings and lights, the Novaks knew this was the handsomest Christmas tree in the world. Grandma sat in the rocking chair, bobbing back and forth. "It is a jewel," she said.

"For a jewel we have a night watchman," Pop said, giving Joe a playful punch on the chest. "And it is time he begins."

"We haven't hung our stockings yet," Anna said.

"Well, hurry then," Mom said. "And then straight to bed. Tomorrow we go to church early, even before it is light, and then to the pastor's kaffeeklatsch."

Because the Novak cottage was small, Joe's bed was the living room couch. Tonight he would be sleeping practically under the tree.

But Joe wasn't sleepy. After the house had settled for the night, he was still excited. He knew there would not be many gifts in the morning. There was no money. Besides, in the Old Country, Christmas had been a church feastday, not a time for giving presents, and his parents followed the customs they had learned in childhood. But to Joe the tree was the big thing. This year, for the first time, he would have a really tall tree to take to the New Year's Eve fire. This year he'd beat old Cousin Karl.

Joe kept his eyes on the dark outline of the tree, trying to make out some of the ornaments glowing faintly in the thick branches. The blue light in the center of the tree would be the gnomes' house. The magic teakettle was a coppery blur in the high branches, alongside the silver bell, which was the oldest ornament, brought by Grandma from the Old Country.

The star at the very tip-top of the tree twinkled like diamonds. It seemed almost as if someone were shaking it. Coaltown was honeycombed with mine tunnels underneath the houses, and because of this, sometimes the earth shifted, yet Joe had not felt such a movement now.

He heard a strange noise, like tissue paper being crushed. It seemed to be coming from the tree. It was kind of scary. Joe burrowed way down under the covers. Soon he was asleep.

On Christmas morning, when Joe awakened, his feet hit the floor immediately, and he rushed to the kitchen. The Novaks had no fireplace, like those all the Christmas ads showed, so Joe and Anna had hung long black stockings, which Grandma had knitted, on pegs alongside the kitchen stove. Pop had banked it for the night, so the room was warm. The stockings were fat and lumpy. Anna came running, tying the belt of her bathrobe, braids flying out behind her. They sat at the table and slowly drew out one treasure after another: hard candies, chocolate drops, cookies shaped like animals, an orange for each. Anna found new clothes for her doll and a rattle to give to the baby.

For Joe there was a pocketknife. He had wanted one for a long time. And now here was this bone-handled whiz of a knife with two shining blades. A boy wasn't a whole boy until he had his own pocketknife. Joe had needed one to cut fishing bait, to carve toy dishes for Anna, to whittle a whistle from a willow twig. Pop had allowed him to use his knife at times, instructing him carefully in its use. "One day, when you know how to handle a knife, you get one of your own," he had said.

Joe heard a noise and turned around. Grandma, Pop, and Mom were in the doorway, smiling. Joe stood up, grinning, holding his knife. He suddenly felt six feet tall.

The pastor's breakfast was a yearly event. He had come from the Rhineland, and always on Christmas morning he invited his parishioners for coffee. They filed down into the holly-garlanded basement hall, buzzing with talk. Tables were ready, laden with *Kaffee Kuchen* and pitchers of hot coffee and cocoa. For each child there was also a sack filled with nuts.

This was a great time for visiting. Always on this morning people began to talk about the New Year's celebrations, which began early New Year's Eve with the Treefire.

Cousin Karl, in a new plaid jacket, two of his

friends alongside, came sliding across the floor
and halted next to Joe. "Hi, Cuz," Karl said,
whacking Joe across the back.

"Hi!" Joe answered.

"Get anything for Christmas?" Karl asked.

Before Joe could answer, Anna piped up. "Joe
got a knife."

That Anna, Joe thought.

Karl's eyes widened. "Seeing's believing," he
said.

Joe pulled the knife out of his trouser pocket. Karl made a grab for it, but Joe was too quick.

"Pretty tight with it, aren't you?" Karl asked. "Well, I'll make you a bet. My printing set, which cost twice as much as your lousy knife, that I bring the biggest tree to the fire."

Joe had no intention of betting his knife. He was silent.

"You're scared to bet 'cause you got a shrimp of a tree as usual," Karl said.

"That's what you think," Joe said.

"Well, put up or shut up. Isn't that so?" Karl asked his friends.

The three of them laughed loudly.

"Bet," Anna whispered. "You'll win."

What did he really stand to lose? Hans Shumaker, the treeman, had said the blue hemlock was the biggest tree on the lot.

"Okay, I'll bet," Joe said.

When they got home, Joe asked Pop again about the New Year's Eve fire. "Why do we burn our trees on New Year's Eve?"

"No one knows exactly how it began," Pop said. "In the days when the mines were working top blast, men came from many countries—Germany, Slovakia, Greece, Ireland. They brought their village traditions to Coaltown. One brought the custom of setting a torch to Christmas trees, and while they blazed, the people joined hands and danced about the fire.

"No one remembers the man, but they remember what he said: 'Christmas trees are sacred, and after all the pleasure they have given, they should not be thrown onto a garbage dump or abandoned in the gutter.'"

"You forget most important part," Grandma chimed in. "If every twig, every pine needle from your tree burn up, then everything will go well through the next year."

Pop's shoulders slumped. "We are in such bad shape here in Coaltown, it will take more than the Treefire to help us."

That night Joe had no more than got under the covers when he heard the crunch-crunch. He sat up, listening. He closed his eyes and listened. He stood up in bed and listened. He put the pillow over his head and listened. The crunch was real. He had not imagined it. It was coming from the tree.

Grandma, her braids loosened from their pins and resting on her shoulders, came to the doorway to say good night. He beckoned to her. "The tree is making a funny noise," he said.

Grandma sat down in the rocker alongside the couch, but she didn't rock. She listened. The

26

crunch-crunch began again. Grandma pursed her lips and nodded her head. "I knew from first this was strange tree."

"It's almost as if the tree is talking," Joe said.

"Long ago my grandfather he tell me that trees stand and listen. They know all the secrets. But he never tell me about talking tree. He did tell me that sometimes the bad sprites capture good sprites and lock them in trees."

Grandma was always ready to tell tales. Joe loved it. "What's a sprite?" he asked.

"Like elf or dwarf, something from fairyland."

Pop came into the room then.

"Listen," Joe said. "There's a sprite in the tree."

Pop listened, but now there was no sound.

"It made a noise like someone was crushing tissue paper," Joe said.

"Aha! A mouse," Pop said. "I must set a trap before your mother hears it. You know how she is about things like that."

"Mouse!" Grandma scoffed. "I bet you don't catch it." She rolled her eyes at Joe and went to bed.

Joe had a silly dream that night. In it crunch-crunch was a language that he could understand. It was spoken by a creature called a Wimp, who was being held captive in the tree by a Wump.

The Wimp was about the size of a clothespin and wore a cap of silver sequins. The Wump looked just like a big dill pickle.

The next morning Grandma was helping Joe smooth out his bed. "Your story about the sprites gave me a nightmare," he told her, and then he related his dream about the good Wimp and the bad Wump.

Grandma didn't laugh. "Dreams can tell us things if we pay attention," she said.

"What was my dream saying?" Joe asked.

28

"I must think about it," Grandma said.

Mom called Joe then and asked him to run an errand. Grandma followed Joe into the kitchen and watched him get into his warm jacket and cap. "Turn around three times," she commanded.

Joe went around in a circle.

"Now sit on chair, and cross legs."

Joe sat. "Why?" he said, chuckling.

"Just in case Wump is around. We hex him before he hex us."

Grandma's eyes were twinkling. It wasn't always possible for Joe to tell when she was joking and when she was serious.

When Joe reached the steep hill near the bridge, he saw that Karl and his friends were sliding down it on flattened pieces of tin. Karl, spinning and whooping, came to a stop at the bottom, then climbed back up. "Hi, Cuz," he said, spying Joe. "Bring your pocketknife? Might as well give it to me now."

Joe grinned. "I'm going to start a newspaper with your printing press. Two cents a copy. I'll be a millionaire."

Karl held out his piece of tin. "Give me the knife now, and you can have this in the bargain. You're going to lose anyway."

"You kidding?" Joe asked. He knew, because Anna had heard it from a friend who had heard it from someone else, that Karl's tree was at least six inches shorter than the blue hemlock. Joe knew his pocketknife was safe. He turned to go. Karl lunged forward and gave him a push. He spun around and headed straight down the icy hill. Miraculously, he kept his feet and reached the bottom still standing up. He couldn't believe it. He turned and looked back up the hill at the open-mouthed Karl and his friends. "I don't need your old tin," he shouted gleefully.

But how had he done it? He'd have to tell Grandma. She'd probably say it was because she put the hex on the bad sprite, that old pickle-faced Wump.

On the way back from Overtown Joe detoured by the clearing where the Treefire would be held. A snowplow had already been at work, and snow was banked high on the sides. A few trees, the runts Hans had not sold probably, were already standing in the center. On the edge of the clearing was the big dead pine used as a marker to tell who had brought the tallest tree. People said that in the olden days there had been a reason for the marker; maybe there had been a prize. No one remembered. Now it was just a matter of rivalry among the boys.

Through the years the boys who had won had carved their initials in the dead trunk. Karl's were there two years running. Joe got out his knife, opened the blades. He itched to carve his initials and the year ahead of time. He made an experimental cut. The blade was keen and true. He put the knife back in his pocket and went on home.

As soon as he came into the house, Grandma called him into the living room, even before he took off his jacket. "What you think, happen, Joe? The bell on the tree rang."

Joe went over to the tree and tapped the silver bell with a finger. "Ting-ting," it sang.

"But, Joe, Anna and I were just sitting here, and it rang all by itself. You heard it, didn't you, Anna?"

Anna, who was dressing her doll, agreed.

"Maybe a truck went by," Joe said.

"We heard nothing. Only the bell. A bell rings for a reason. In the Old Country it rings for church or to call people to tell them something important."

"Crunch-crunch-crunch," came from the tree.

"You know what it sound like?" Grandma asked. "It sound like someone is calling: '*Help, help, help.*'"

Joe listened. It did sort of sound like that. He grinned. "Maybe it's my Wimp begging us to get him out of the clutches of the Wump."

Anna giggled. "You use funny words," she said.

She went around making a song of them: "Wimp-Wump, Wimpety-Wump, Wumpety-Wimp."

The next night, when supper was over and the family was still at the table, Pop smiled at Joe. "Well, I did not find any work today Overtown, but I learned something about the tree. I talked to a man who once worked in the forests, and he said that a paint mark on a tree could mean it was not to be cut."

"I know why," Anna butted in. "Because there's a Wimp in the tree. It talks to Grandma, and it rings the bell. Wimp-Wump, Wimpety-Wump—"

Pop frowned. "Stop such foolish talk," he said, and then he went on. "The man said the mark might be because the tree is infested with the pine borer and so is to be treated or maybe even destroyed if there is danger of infecting other trees. I think we now know what made the noise."

Mom's eyes widened. "You mean there is a worm in our living room eating up the tree?"

Pop nodded. "Could be."

Mom got up from the table and hurried into the living room. They all followed. *"Crunch-Crunch,"* the tree said.

"There *is* a worm in the tree. Maybe many worms," Pop said.

"I can almost see their jaws moving," Mom said.

Grandma's eyes flashed. "First you say mouse. Now worm. All because of something you do not understand."

"Wimp-Wump, Wimpety-Wump," Anna sang.

Pop frowned at Grandma. "I have had enough of this Wimp-Wump business."

Mom, who was brave about big things like thunder and lightning and spooks, was afraid of silly things like bugs and mice. "It makes me shiver," she said.

Pop looked from Anna to Joe. "I know it is early to take the tree down, but why not give the birds a Christmas tree? We will leave the popcorn and cranberries on the branches."

"The cookies, too," Mom said. "We can't eat cookies off a wormy tree."

Joe expected Anna to make a fuss. But Anna was like Mom. She backed away from the tree. "Worms," she said, making a face.

"How about it, Joe?" Pop asked.

"Okay," he said.

But he was sorry. He enjoyed listening to Grandma's tales about sprites and elves. Sometimes he half-believed them. It was fun to believe.

Mom brought in the empty boxes for the ornaments.

"Well, now we start," Pop said. "Who wants to take off the first ornament?"

33

"I do, I do," Anna cried.

At that very moment the silver bell began to tinkle. They watched as it fell from branch to branch, tinkling all the way down to the floor, where it crashed into a mound of silver splinters.

It had been their favorite. Everyone helped gather up the pieces. Everyone but Grandma. She sat in the rocker, rocking back and forth, her arms crossed over her chest, her eyes on the tree. She was usually in the thick of things when there was work to be done. But tonight she didn't remove a single ornament.

Joe wondered if she felt sad about the bell. He remembered now what she had said: "A bell rings for a reason."

The next day she spent much time at the window watching the birds having their feast. Joe watched, too, when he wasn't carving things with his knife. One of the birds kept flying to the windowsill, perching there, looking up at them.

"Birds know things," Grandma said. "This one wants to tell us something."

Joe did not remind Grandma that she often put crumbs on the windowsill for the birds. She had a faraway look in her eyes now as she spoke. "The strange yellow mark, the crunch, the tinkling bell, your dream, would all have been taken as warnings in the Old Country."

"Of what?" Joe asked.

"That the tree must be saved."

Joe fingered his knife. The tree *had* to go to the fire.

"I remember now," Grandma said. "It suddenly comes to me. They said in the Old Country that sprites could free themselves in water. Joe, maybe that is what the Wimp was telling us."

"We can't help it," Joe said.

"Faith gives a man four hands," Grandma said.

Grandma was going too far. He would not listen to her anymore. He wanted to talk to Pop, who didn't believe in such things. Pop had gone Overtown about work. Joe decided to find him.

The weather had turned warmer. The sun felt good on Joe's face. Snow was melting, and there was no longer ice on the sidewalks. Joe noticed all these things on his walk Overtown, but what he noticed most was the men standing around the streets with nothing to do but talk. He stood up against the front of the post office, watching for Pop, listening to the men: "The town is dead. Better we bury it on New Year's instead of having celebrations." "We will all have to leave to find work elsewhere unless there is a miracle." "Miracle. Haw!"

Poor Grandma. Joe guessed she was probably the only one who believed in such things.

He saw his father and Cousin Alex coming down the street, and he hurried to join them. Pop

put a hand on Joe's shoulder, but the men kept on talking as they walked along.

"What will you do about the family?" Uncle Alex asked.

"I cannot afford to move them now. Maybe later," Pop said.

"I will see if there is room in my boardinghouse for you," Cousin Alex said.

So now Joe knew the worst. Pop was really going away. He felt a lump in his throat, and his eyes began to sting. He slipped away and started for home.

When he went around to the backyard, a great many birds were whirling about the tree. Some were in the branches, and others were dive-bombing over it. He stopped to watch. It did seem to Joe that the birds were acting strangely. He went close to the tree, and the birds took off. He listened, but he could not hear the crunch-crunch. He looked up and saw Grandma watching at the window. He wondered what it would be like to believe as she did. Joe liked to play pretend, so now he pretended he did believe. All he had to do was get the tree to water, the river maybe, and then the good Wimp would free itself and the bad Wump would not have his way with the town. He'd lose his pocketknife, but now he invented a pretend game about that. Pop would get full-time work, and so would all the men in Coaltown. The shops would be busy, and they would be glad to hire Joe to shovel snow off their sidewalks. Soon he'd have enough to buy another knife.

The game was so good and so convincing that Joe reached out, grabbed the trunk of the tree, and lifted it to see how heavy it was and whether he could throw it over the bridge.

Just then he heard the squeak of rubbers on snow. Pop came around the path. He walked right up to Joe and began talking as if he understood everything in Joe's mind. "You must understand, son, that Grandma lives in the past. When she was a child, almost everyone believed in little people and omens. It was so in almost every country. But not here. We never believed in such things in the new land. Tomorrow morning you and I will carry the tree to the clearing for the New Year's Eve fire. If we have nothing else, we still have the biggest tree. And you will carve your initials in the marker. Forever after, when you are a grown man even, you can point to it and say, 'In this year I had the tallest tree in Coaltown.'"

Joe looked back at the window. Grandma was still there. He hoped she understood that he had tried to save the tree. Secretly he was glad Pop had stopped him. He was glad because of the pocket-knife.

Just as Joe was waking up the next morning, he heard Anna's loud shrieks coming from the kitchen. He rushed out in his pajamas. Grandma and Mom were at the window with Anna, who was pointing. "The tree is gone. Someone stole the tree," she cried.

Joe thought he must still be dreaming. He rubbed his eyes. The yard was a blanket of snow. There was no Christmas tree. Hadn't Pop trusted him? Had he taken the tree himself?

"Someone stole our tree," Anna cried again.

"Did Pop take it?" Joe asked Mom.

"No. He left early to meet Cousin Alex and make arrangements about the city. Anna is right. Someone must have stolen it."

Joe wanted to kick a chair or hit his fists into the wall. Now he didn't even have a tree. He would lose his pocketknife. Everything was turning out wrong.

Grandma hadn't said anything. She went to the stove and poured herself a mug of coffee. "It looks as if tree was dragged through the snow. Put your clothes on, Joe, and follow the mark. Perhaps you discover something."

Joe hurried to dress. He put on his sweater, his cap with the earflaps, and his boots and went outside. He took a close look at the drag mark and the footsteps. The footsteps puzzled him because they did not seem to be a boy's or a man's. He glanced back at the kitchen window and saw that Grandma was watching, and now he knew who had dragged the tree. Grandma was the one with four hands.

The marks led directly to the forbidden wood that belonged to the Old Man. Joe was afraid to enter, but Grandma had not been, so he followed her footsteps, his heart pounding. Through the bare trees he glimpsed the big house on the hill. Its top story had a cupola that looked out over the village. People said that when the Old Man lived here, he saw everything that happened in Coal-town.

Joe had not gone far into the trees before he saw the blue hemlock. It stood right alongside the path. "Well, hello there," Joe said, and he felt as if he'd met an old friend. He listened for the crunch-crunch but couldn't hear it.

Well, he had his tree. He could take it to the clearing and have the tallest tree at the fire. He could carve his name on the marker. But now he did not want to. Grandma had been so sure the tree was magic, he had to save it for her sake. He knew there was a way to reach the river through these woods. He began to drag the tree along the path. There was so much snow it was hard to fol-low the route through the trees. He had not gone very far before he was lost. He stopped to catch his breath.

It was then he heard a twig snap. He turned. A stranger, in a greatcoat lined with fur, stood there. He wore a fur cap with earflaps, but some of his thick silver hair was visible. His dark eyes were blazing.

"You are on private property. Didn't you see the sign?"

"Yes, but—"

"The sign warns that you will be prosecuted if you walk on this land. Do you know what that means?"

"Jail," Joe squeaked.

"Then what are you doing here?"

"I'm trying to reach the river so I can put my Christmas tree into it."

"Why?" the man thundered.

"I don't want it to be burned."

"That's the proper end for Christmas trees," the man shouted. "Take the tree back where you came from, and don't let me see you here again."

"I can't," Joe said.

"What was that?" the man growled.

"My grandmother believes a sprite lives in this tree," Joe stumbled on. "You won't believe it. Nobody does. But in the Old Country, where she

41

came from, elves and dwarfs and fairies lived in the woods."

The man didn't move, and Joe went on to tell him the whole story. "I know my grandmother believes that if I don't rescue the sprite, times will get even harder in Coaltown, the Old Man who owns the mines will never open them, and my Pop will have to go to the city to work."

Joe was close to tears now, and he rubbed his eyes with his sleeve.

"I see," the man said, and he sat down on the stump of a tree. "Do you know, I had a grandmother like that? She believed. And why shouldn't our grandmothers be right?"

"My grandmother says faith is like having four hands," Joe said.

"And that's just what you need to get this tree to the river. It's a bit uphill part of the way, and you're off the path. How about letting me help? For *my* grandmother."

The man took hold of the blue hemlock at the big end and led the way, while Joe grasped its tip.

They walked through the trees, up a snowy hill, to a rocky knoll. Below the river coursed south. Joe had been afraid it would be frozen, but it wasn't. Together they rolled the tree off the high place.

"There goes our sprite, off to save us all," the man said.

I believe! I believe! Joe thought, and he tingled

43

with excitement as he watched the tree make a big splash in the water.

"Good luck," the man shouted at the bobbing tree.

Joe watched it out of sight around a bend in the river. "So long, Wimp," he cried.

When Joe turned around, the man was gone.

When Joe reached his backyard, it was noon. Everything was the same. Gone was the magic he had felt on the hill. His spirits fell. For that one thrilling moment, when he and the man had started the tree on its journey, he would have to give up his pocketknife.

Why had he been so stupid as to believe there could be something magic about a tree? He stood in the yard, in the spot where the tree had been, and closed his eyes. He wanted to believe, to re-capture the excitement of the knoll.

Suddenly a whistle shrilled through the village.

Pop came running outside in his shirt sleeves. Mom and Grandma stood at the door.

"It can't be," Pop said.

"It's the mine whistle," Mom said.

"There she goes again," Pop said. "Three blasts. The call to the mine office."

Mom held Pop's jacket for him. Grandma handed him his cap. He hurried out front. Joe ran

after him to the street. Already men were rushing from the other cottages, shouting, heading Overtown.

That night the villagers stood in lively groups at the edge of the clearing, talking excitedly about the events of the day. Mom and Pop, carrying the baby, were with some of the relations, Cousin Alex included. The Old Man had personally talked to the men this noon and discussed new ways and means of operating the mines. He had promised that the mines would open right after New Year's. "He was always one to keep his promises," Alex reminded.

Joe didn't have a tree for the fire, and he knew he must give up his pocketknife. But he was bursting with smiles as he watched Grandma and Anna join hands when it came time to put a torch to the mountain of Christmas trees.

Joe expected his Cousin Karl to come gloating, his tough companions in tow. But Karl came alone.

"Here," Joe said, pulling the pocketknife from his trouser pocket.

Karl took it sheepishly. "You can use it anytime you want," he said.

"Oh, I'll get another," Joe said.

"You will?" Karl asked. "Where?"

"From a fellow I know called a Wimp," Joe said.

"There's no such person," Karl said.

"There is if you believe there is," Joe said.

"Say, there's the fire. Let's get into the circle," Karl said, extending his hand.

It was the best New Year's celebration yet. The fire whooshed its way clear to the stars. Or so it seemed to Joe.

The Author

DALE FIFE lives with her family in San Mateo, California, where she spends a good deal of time writing. She is the author of both adult novels and stories for boys and girls.

Dale Fife's other books for young readers are *A Stork for the Bell Tower*, *A Dog Called Dunkel*, *Fish in the Castle*, *Who's in Charge of Lincoln?* and *Walk a Narrow Bridge*, for which she received the 1967 juvenile award presented by the Martha Kinney Cooper Ohioana Library Association.